To everyone who likes the ballet—A.G.

For Mum and Dad—S.M.

DIAL BOOKS FOR YOUNG READERS

A division of Penguin Young Readers Group

Published by The Penguin Group

Penguin Group (USA) Inc., 375 Hudson Street, New York, NY 10014, U.S.A.

Penguin Group (Canada), 90 Eglinton Avenue East, Suite 700, Toronto, Ontario, Canada M4P 2Y3 (a division of Pearson Penguin Canada Inc.)

Penguin Books Ltd, 80 Strand, London WC2R 0RL, England

Penguin Ireland, 25 St. Stephen's Green, Dublin 2, Ireland (a division of Penguin Books Ltd)

Penguin Group (Australia), 250 Camberwell Road, Camberwell, Victoria 3124, Australia (a division of Pearson Australia Group Pty Ltd)

Penguin Books India Pvt Ltd, 11 Community Centre, Panchsheel Park, New Delhi - 110 017, India

Penguin Group (NZ), Cnr Airborne and Rosedale Roads, Albany, Auckland 1310, New Zealand (a division of Pearson New Zealand Ltd)

Penguin Books (South Africa) (Pty) Ltd, 24 Sturdee Avenue, Rosebank, Johannesburg 2196, South Africa

Penguin Books Ltd, Registered Offices: 80 Strand, London WC2R 0RL, England

First published in the United States 2008 by

Dial Books for Young Readers

Published in Great Britain 2007 by

Orchard Books

Text copyright © 2007 by Adèle Geras

Pictures copyright © 2007 by Shelagh McNicholas

All rights reserved

The publisher does not have any control over and does not assume any responsibility for author or third-party websites or their content.

Printed in Singapore

1 3 5 7 9 10 8 6 4 2

Library of Congress Cataloging-in-Publication Data available upon request

Little Ballet Star

by Adèle Geras

illustrated by Shelagh McNicholas

Dial Books for Young Readers

I'm so excited, I could burst! Today is my birthday and
I'm going to the theater to see a ballet from the fairy tale
The Sleeping Beauty. My aunt Gina is a ballerina and
she's taking me backstage before the show as a special treat.

Backstage, some of the dancers are practicing their steps.

"If you put on your ballet shoes, you can join in,"
says Aunt Gina.

I love my ballet shoes. They make my feet feel sparkly.

I do my pliés,

and point my toes
just exactly right.

I twirl and spin. Everyone claps!

Aunt Gina takes me to the dressing room.
Three ballerinas are putting on makeup.

One of them strokes some blusher onto my cheeks.
I look like a pink apple!

Then we go up to the wardrobe department, where the costumes are kept.

"Happy birthday, Tilly," says Margie,
the wardrobe mistress.
"Would you like to try this on?"
"Ooh, so pretty!" I say. "Yes, please!"

She helps me into
a real fairy costume,

and I twirl in front
of the mirror.

Next, we go downstairs.
"These are the wings where the dancers wait
until it's time to go on stage," says Aunt Gina.
I tip-tip-tiptoe in my pink shoes.

The stage is *so* big and the lights are dazzle-bright!
They make me blink and feel hot. The scenery is a huge
beautiful painting of Sleeping Beauty's fairy-tale palace.
It almost looks real.

I can hear music coming from behind the curtains.
I sneak a peak at the orchestra tuning their instruments,
making funny noises before they play
real music.

The rows of seats are filling up with people,
and I can see Mom!
Aunt Gina says, "The ballet is about to start, Tilly.
You can sit with your mom to watch the show."

Mom asks me if I've had a good time and I start to tell her about it, but then the lights go down . . .

I'm so excited, I can hardly breathe. Music fills the whole theater. It feels like something magical is about to happen.

Then the fairies run onto the stage! They're wearing their pretty tutus. And there's Aunt Gina!

Aunt Gina is the most important ballerina of all—
she's Sleeping Beauty! Her headdress has pale lilac
roses on it, and her tutu glitters and sparkles.
The music makes me want to dance too!

Everyone claps when the ballet is finished, but I clap the loudest. I wish I could see it all over again.

Then Aunt Gina steps through the closed curtains and comes to the front of the stage.

"We have a birthday girl in the audience today," she says, "and it just so happens that she's a little ballerina. Come up here, Tilly, darling!"

I'm going up there!
Up on stage!

The curtains open again and Aunt Gina says,
"Let's do a special birthday dance together."

I've got butterflies in my tummy!

Then the music starts
and I'm dancing,

and twirling,

and flitting,

and floating.

I want to shout,
"I'm dancing on a real stage!
I'm dancing like a real ballerina!"

Then the orchestra plays "Happy Birthday" and I do my very best curtsey ever.

Everyone claps and claps.
I'm so happy, I could jump!

Aunt Gina gives me her headdress.
"A birthday present for you, Tilly,"
she says. "You're a wonderful ballerina."

I give her a big hug and say, "Thank you, Aunt Gina."

Dad's waiting for Mom and me outside the theater.

He picks me up and carries me all the way to the car.

Beauty

STAGE DOOR

"I'm very tired," I say as I close my eyes.

"You're our very own Sleeping Beauty," says Dad.

I'm going to dream of the ballet tonight—I just know I am.